THE STORY OF US

A novel

Paul M. Polynice

THE STORY OF US

A novel

Translated from French by Garry F. Doxy
www.labalanguageservices.com

Cover artwork copyright
© 2020 Pascale Doxy. *Our Love* (detail)

ISBN: 978-0-578-24524-9

Printed in the U.S.A by Lulu Press, Inc.
January 2021

FORWARD

The Story of Us (Histoire de Nous) is a little story I wrote in the 90s. It is an almost true fiction inspired by youthful souvenirs…

I am grateful to my niece Pascale for believing and giving life to it some twenty years later.

So…

to Pascale

Chapter 1

In the neighborhood of Christ-Roi lived the Bourjoly family. The Bourjolys had three children: Gertrude, Naomie, and Scott. Naomie, the middle-child, lived at a Catholic boarding school, the Sisters of the Sacré-Coeur de Turgeau...

The Bourjoly's home was one of those old beautiful gingerbread houses that still adorned Port-au-Prince at that time. It was carefully maintained with little modification added. The red painted house was in the middle of a garden and was ornated with white balustrade all around. After a day of activities, the porch that made the tour of the house was often where the whole family gathered. Each Sunday, it was there the children entertained their friends with laughter and jokes. It was also there that the craziest projects came to life.

The sky was bright and the air was the purest on a Saturday afternoon. Gertrude, while sitting on the porch, was finishing the last pages of a novel. Suddenly, a car's loud noise stopped just in front of the house. It was a taxi dropping off Naomie. Every year, around Easter break, she came back home for a few days.

Gertrude saw Naomie and leaped out of her rocking chair and shouted to everyone that Naomie has arrived and rushed to meet her. She was welcomed and immediately relieved of her luggage which were put in her room. The joy of her arrival transformed the entire family that afternoon and everyone was eating, talking, and going back-and-forth with a bit of conversation in between here and there. Meanwhile, Naomie did not have a chance to rest.

She went straight to the flower garden. No one couldn't resist the temptation. As always, everyone passing by couldn't continue walking through without admiring the colorful roses and the inviting smell of the odorous jasmines. Mrs. Bourjoly was a very serious gardener. Naomie called her jokingly the "guardian" of her garden.

Naomie resembled her mother in many ways. Not only she had the same marabout complexion and tiny height, she also shared the same passion for horticulture. She was very happy to see the blossoming flowers and to discover a few tulips that her mother added to the display…

Diner was ready. As customary, Mr. Bourjoly said a prayer. Then, the fish and the salad that Gertrude prepared disappeared quickly. Between bites, Mrs. Bourjoly asked Naomie:

"Naomie, you are going to church with us tomorrow morning, right?"

"Of course, mother."

"Me, I'm not going," said Scott.

"And why young man?" asked Mr. Bourjoly.

"I don't feel well…" answered Scott with a weird face.

"Come on Scott!" said Naomie. "You don't want to go to church because, you don't want to miss your favorite program on TV. That's it, right?"

"What program? I really don't feel well," insisted Scott.

Mrs. Bourjoly looked straight in the eyes of her son before touching his forehead.

"With all the wind these days, it must be a cold coming on," she finally said. "I will make some Hibiscus tea with honey and you'll be good as new tomorrow."

Scott leaned in on his plate without saying a word. He was happy to see his mother take his side.

At thirteen, he was as tall as his father. He was proud of that. However, he was smart enough to understand to never cross his mother if he wanted some of his schemes to come to fruition. Every time he did not want to go to church, he would fake a sickness. But he knew to spread them around between several months so as to not get caught.

After drinking two cups of the tea, Scott went to bed early that night. The next day will be a special day for him. Usually, he meets up with his friend André, who was barely twelve-year old, living across his house. They were inseparable friends. They both loved to invent stories to avoid going to mass.

Next day came and everyone woke up at six in the morning. The sound of the church bells resounded in the distance. Everyone was getting ready. To support his ruse, Scott stood facing the rising sun for a few good minutes. The sun's heat would elevate his core temperature, just in case his mother would come to check on him.

In his blueish-grey suit, Mr. Bourjoly waited impatiently. He asked Naomie where was Scott. He did not notice him in the bustling of the house.

"Scott," answered a smiling Naomie, "is still sleeping. Mom's tea must have been too strong."

"He's still sleeping!" yelled Mr. Bourjoly. "That's impossible! What a lazy child! I need to start handling this boy. We're going to let him have his way today. We must get there on time to find seats or we'll be standing the whole ceremony."

The church was not far though. The Bourjolys often went on foot. On the way, they would exchange greetings with people they encountered. Almost everyone knew each other in the neighborhood.

Mr. Bourjoly was right. The ceremony was already in full swing when they arrived, but they managed to find seats near an entrance.

On the other side almost facing the Bourjolys stood a handsome young man. He was tall, slender, chiseled face, wearing a blue suit. He was not as lucky. He looked for a seat but all were already taken. He was cloistered in the arch of one of the large lateral doors. This young man was Palomino Leroi. Well educated and very religious, Palomino was a Good Samaritan who loved everyone. He never missed a Sunday mass.

The liturgy was following its course with the hymns and all when a distinctive voice tingled Palomino's hear. It was a sweet floating voice leaving below the others. Palomino lifted his head buried in his hymnals and reviewed the chorus. His eyes stopped at the harmonious face of Naomie. Palomino was captivated and charmed. The overall graciousness of voice and person fixed his gaze. It was a welcomed surprise: a sweet and angelic voice. For the first time, Palomino felt something he never experienced before…

Completely invested in her singing, Naomie was unaware of what was developing under the nave. Innocently a little later, she looked at the parishioners. Her eyes crossed that of Palomino. He was still staring at her. Naomie lowered her head timidly. But during all the ceremony, from the corner of her eyes, she monitored and felt the persistent gaze of the young man. She was intrigued. Despite her shyness, she could not resist the desire to look at him. Once again, their eyes met and… Naomie smiled…

Palomino's face brightened. Yes, often a little smile says a lot more than an I love you... Before they could talk to each other both felt a deep connection...

Meanwhile, just after his family left, Scott went to a drawer and took out a small bag full with pins and a few strings. He left the house cautiously making sure no one saw him. He made a signal and quickly André, his friend, appeared at the window of his bedroom across the street. He came out also as discreetly as possible. The friends headed to the church, the scene of the day's experiment. Midway, Scott asked André:

"Are you well equipped?"

"Yes," answered André. "And you, do you have the pins? How many?"

"I think I have a dozen or so," answered Scott. "And you know, this morning, I found some strings in my drawer. I took them just in case."

"Good idea! If we don't have enough pins, we could tie them with the strings like rabid dogs!"

They laughed so hard that anyone could hear them at a distance. As soon as Scott and André arrived at the church, they got to work. Methodically and in the utmost silence, they tied together the late comers standing in front of the church. Fully concentrated on the priest giving the Eucharist, these folks were oblivious to what was happening behind them.

Having tied them up perfectly half an hour later, Scott and André rested in a corner of the church's courtyard. They spoke in a low voice. They laughed waiting patiently to see the fruit of their labor.

Mass continued. The people's sung and prayed. Finally, Father Camille blessed the parishioners and said:

"Go in peace!"

Slowly, people were leaving. After a few polite exchanges, the Bourjolys left the nave. The crowd of parishioners slowly moved toward the doors.

Naomie's heart looked for the blue-wearing young man's eye. But the crowd made it difficult to see. Leaving, she looked several times if Palomino was behind her. No, he wasn't. She then thought that he was not really interested in her. She went away sad.

But if only she knew what situation Palomino was in…From where he was standing, a group of people tied to each other were quarrelling. They could not go forward or backward. Those going forward were dragging involuntarily those tied to them. Palomino was amused despite of himself. Quickly, he realized he was in the same situation. His amused smiled turned into frustration because untying himself from the lady standing near him took longer

11

than he might have wanted. How would he now find the beautiful young mademoiselle and present himself to the family?

An abrupt movement torn a piece of his clothing and freed him. The lady made a horrifying noise thinking she had the tearing lost. She hit Palomino with her bag. He excused himself and quickly left the scene.

He was free, free to run to the entrance to see if Naomie was there. It was too late. He searched the church's courtyard. She was gone. Palomino was disappointed with the unfolding events. Finally, he decided to go home. He would have liked to find some information on the young woman! But how! No name, no photo, what to do? He had so many conflicting thoughts. He sighed. Compare to his shirt, the world has not ended yet. There was still hope. He regained his courage in thinking that maybe next Sunday he could see her again at the same place, at the same time…

Sunday came and he made his way happily to the church, certain he will meet her again... He eagerly looked for her but she was not there. Was she late? Half hour later, he was still waiting. He examined each row of seats, the late comers, the entrances, and the church's courtyard – still no Naomie.

Many months passed but Palomino was unfazed in his quest. He went from church to church, neighborhood to neighborhood, theatre to theatre, here and there to find her, even if by chance. But he was looking in vain for Naomie returned to the boarding school a few days after their first encounter at the church...

Chapter 2

Naomie, also, had thoughts of Palomino. She did not forget the handsome young man of the church, nor the fleshly lips that made his smile, or his deep gaze framed by thick and well-drawn eyebrows.

To whom could she confide her thoughts? Even her childhood friend, Joséphine, would call her crazy. What would she think of falling in love with a stranger upon meeting his distant gaze, of whom nothing is known, and whom has not been seen since!

Naomie loved music and singing. When she was thinking of Palomino, the boarding school's piano became her only confident. One evening, the neighborhood witnessed one of those sentimental moments. The piano was sounding melancholically Lionel Richie's song *Hello…*

The boarding school was on Palomino's usual route. That evening the well-executed notes attracted his attention. The illuminated compound, nestled by high walls, was impenetrable. Only the metal bars of the gate allowed someone to have a glimpse of the activities inside the imposing boarding school. Inexplicably, Palomino peered in. An opened window showed the profile of a young woman playing the beautiful music.

"My God!" Palomino could not believe his eyes. This young woman, could she be the one he was looking for? His heart racing, Palomino stayed glued to the gate.

Noise of coming steps brought him back to reality. Not wanting to be caught peering inside this woman's boarding school, he took a small street that followed the property line. He bent down to tie his shoe laces. A bell rang and the piano stopped. Palomino raced back. He slowly walked in front of the compound at the exact moment the gate was opening. A young woman wearing a dress similar to the piano player appeared. Palomino examined her from head to toe. No, it was not her. He headed home sadder than before.

*

A few days later, Palomino witnessed a few students fighting after school. Seeing him coming, the bullies ran away leaving a bloody boy on the ground. Palomino asked the boy his name. He did not respond. Palomino assumed the situation to be serious and called a taxi. He brought the boy to the nearest clinic but was unable to answer the many questions of the medical staff regarding the boy. The boy was a perfect little stranger to him. But he did not want to leave him. In his heart, he asked God for the boy's recovery.

As God is not hard of hearing, the boy slowly opened his eyes. Palomino sighed in relief. The boy felt strange and uneasy.

"Where am I?" he asked. "Who brought me here?"

He turned toward Palomino. In his eyes were confusion and fright. Palomino extended his hand and said:

"I am Palomino. And you?"

"Me, me I'm Scott. Scott Bourjoly."

"Scott Bourjoly? A nice name…This morning I found you on the ground. I didn't want to leave you there. That's why you're at the doctor's office."

"Oh, thank you."

"And why? We're all fellow human."

"You know," said Scott. "I haven't gone home yet. My parents must be very anxious now…"

"I see…You have a telephone number I could call for you?"

"Yes, but the phone hasn't worked for a few weeks now…"

"Then, how about your address?"

"I live on Odain street - 312 Odain street."

"I think I know where that is. It's not far from my house. Don't worry now. You're in good hands. I'll let your parents know. I'll be back. Ok?"

Grateful for Palomino's kindness, The Bourjolys welcomed him open arms. Added that his elegance, education, and bravery supported his worthiness. Mr. Bourjoly developed an affectionate bond with the young man. They spent many Sunday afternoons discussing news events.

"It's revolting to see what has become of this country!" cried out Mr. Bourjoly one day. "Beating people just because they're protesting!"

"It's even sadder," said Palomino, "when as a journalist, you travel all around and you discover how much injustice is sickening our dear Haiti."

"One thing is certain," said Mr. Bourjoly, "1983 will be famous in history."

Palomino was an activist. His work offered him the possibility to travel the entire country in search of instances of oppression, total misery, inacceptable disparity. His faith had also sharpened his sense of justice.

"*Mezanmi*!" (Beware!) cried out softly Mrs. Bourjoly, "you all want them to come for us? Stop this conversation right now."

"Mom," said Scott, "you're afraid of everything."

"Mom is right," intervened Gertrude her eyes showing a little concern. "Why won't we talk about Haiti's participation in the Maja International. What do you think Mom if I participated next year in the competition as Miss Haiti?"

"No, my daughter. Focus on your secretary studies."

Mr. Burjoly and Palomino exchanged an amused look while Scott was rolling back his eyes laughing.

It was just like that, slowly, Palomino became like a son. During all his visits to the family, Palomino did not know he was at his beloved home and less that the boy he helped was Naomie's little brother…

*

At the begin of the following year, Naomie told her parents that she would love to celebrate her 18th birthday with them. A few days later, Palomino, Joséphine, Samuel, Gertrude's fiancé, were on the veranda.

"Gertrude, what do you think?" Asked Joséphine. "Isn't a good time to reunite all our friends here?"

"It's a good idea!" answered Gertrude "But let's ask the parents first. If they agree, I'll invite the Bayards, Etheards, Delisforts, Bertrands, Calixtes, Victors and more…"

"Yes…with them the party will be more grandiose", supported Joséphine."

"And you Palomino?" Gertrude asked. "This time you're coming with your fiancée right?"

"Ah, Gertrude! How many times I told you I don't have a fiancée…The only fiancée I would like to bring is nowhere to be found."

"What do you mean nowhere to be found?" asked a puzzled Gertrude.

"It's a girl I saw at church a few months ago. Oh! That girl! You should have seen her! She had a soft voice and so beautiful that I couldn't take my eyes off of her. During the ceremony, our eyes would meet. She gave me a little smile. And I couldn't forget her…"

"Did you try to find her?" Samuel asked.

"I have hoped to meet her that day when leaving the church. But strangely, I don't know how, someone tied people together. I could not leave."

"Really? I heard of that story," said a smiling Gertrude. "You were among the tied folks?"

"Yes. I missed her because of that. Since, I can't find her."

"Ah…That's unfortunate," Gertrude sighed. "Don't be discouraged. Maybe someday you'll find her."

"I hope…"

The day of the anticipated party came quickly. The courtyard, the veranda, the living room were decorated with yellow ribbons - Naomie's favorite color. A few balloons attached to the house's poles finished the decorations. The dining room table was filled with sugary, salty, and deliciously seared dishes, sandwiches, and hors-d'oeuvres.

Mr. Bourjoly was the bar tender to stop, as he said, "the excesses". Mrs. Bourjoly was coming and going between the kitchen and the dining room because she wanted to make sure the table was always full of goodies. Everything was done to make this party memorable.

The Larieux and Etheard families arrived. The Bayards and the Calixtes were already there. Everyone was just waiting for Naomie to start the festivities.

Naomie was in her bedroom getting ready. She got out a white lace dress from her closet. She put on a light rosy makeup and her favorite fruity perfume.

A few minutes later, with a smile, Naomie left her room and like a queen slowly made her way to the guests. Upon seeing her, all got up and shouted "Bonne Anniversaire".

Oh! How beautiful! What joy!

Meanwhile, where was Palomino? He was not rushed. It was a busy day for him. Several times, he even thought of not going.

He knew a Bourjoly was coming from a boarding school to celebrate her anniversary. But he had no thought of finding out who that Bourjoly really was. Finally, he put on a white shirt, khaki pants, and left his house.

Spread all over, guests were happily enjoying themselves when Palomino arrived. Mr. Bourjoly hurried him in and presented him to a cercle of friends.

"You're coming just now?" Gertrude asked with reproach in her voice.

"Not at all. It's been half an hour since I came."

"Really? We were waiting for you to start singing *"Bonne Anniversaire"* to my sister. But you were not there. Where were you?"

Not knowing what to say in defense, Palomino smiled and shrugged his shoulders.

The living room doubled as a dance floor. A panel full of mirrors, on one of the walls, was reflecting the likeness of the dancing guests. It was on one of the mirrors the queenly Naomie saw a reflection of Palomino. The young woman stopped, her eyes widening. She started to tremble.

"My God!" she said to herself.

Naomie stood there and stared at the reflection. She was convinced that she was dreaming. But Palomino seemed real. He was drinking, moving, and talking to Gertrude. She could no longer control her emotions. She went back to her room crying tears of joy…

"Oh!" Gertrude remembered. "You haven't met my sister Naomie yet.

"Not yet."

"Come quickly present yourself," commanded Gertrude while dragging him toward the veranda.

Naomie wasn't there. Gertrude looked for her everywhere and finally found her in her bedroom.

"Naomie!" she cried out. "What are you doing here by yourself? It's your party. You should be with everyone…"

Naomie barely lifted her head. She made an effort to smile and recomposed herself.

"Well! Never mind"… Gertrude continued not noticing anything. "This is Palomino I told you about. It was him that

27

saved our little brother Scott. Present yourself."

Gertrude signaled Palomino to come closer. He was standing a little bit far behind. Upon seeing Naomie, Palomino muffled a surprise sound. A joyful spark started the dormant fire in his heart and it was already singing.

Naomie could not believe it either. Her heart was exploding. To meet like this, face to face, in the flesh, inexplicably! Trembling, Palomino extended his hand and stammered:

"Would you like to dance?"

Without saying a word, the young woman put her hand in Palomino's and both followed the music in the living room.

Gertrude watched them going amazed at what she was seeing not knowing that she was the first witness of this story.

Passing in front of the DJ, Naomie had the presence of mind to ask for a song: "*L'Étranger*"…

Naomie and Palomino seemed to be made for each other. Everyone conceded the floor to the lovers. The light from the chandelier reflected on the face of the waltzing Naomie an unparallel happiness. She was stunning in her white dress. She was stunning in her movement. One would have said she was a falling angel…

Oh, how many times has she dreamt of being in the arms of the one she loves so! Palomino matched her elegance and supple steps. To them, nothing else existed.

After the dance, they rushed away to the garden to get better acquainted. They had so much to say to each other. Time was not enough to express their joy, emotions, love…

The garden listened and helped in their first conversation. The roses, the birds

29

dictated the words of love. Naomie's fruity perfume further subdued Palomino's heart. The emptiness that time had dug in their souls was being filled by the present intimacy. They could no longer leave each other…

Chapter 3

It took the pair no time to envision a blissful future together. They could be seen everywhere: at the beach, at the theatre, and at the movies. They were made for each other.

Naomie had her national exams to pass and Mrs. Bourjoly feared her daughter would fail because of this romance. Naomie aced the tests with honors while dreaming of happiness. Palomino wanted to wed without delay. But their financial situation did not allow for an immediate union. They had to wait…

At the beginning of summer, Naomie left the boarding school and came home.

She was happy to tend to the garden. Palomino helped her to plant new roses and tulips around the house. With this tender care, like the roses their love blossomed.

"My love," said Palomino, "what if we name this beautiful garden."

"We could call it... *Garden of Lovers*. What do you think?"

Palomino touched gently Naomie's face.

"Yes," he said to her in a soft voice. "That's a great idea."

They stood there for a while admiring the garden and holding on to each other. Time had no meaning. A few months went by like this. They were more and more bonded by the strength of love. Everything was going well until days of insecurity fell on the country.

Ah! *Manman pitit mare vant!* (Mothers gird yourselves!)

Oh! How many killed in the streets! How many innocents died! It was a carnage! Palomino denounced more and more these atrocities in his paper. He could not stay indifferent to the suffering of his countrymen. How many parents, how many close friends disappeared, killed by death squads because they dared break the silence…

Palomino's visits to the Bourjolys became rare by necessity. A few brief conversations on the phone, a few letters delivered by trusted friends were Naomie's sole consolations during those turbulent moments. Life had become perilous for their love.

Palomino had no choice. The government wanted his life.

"You must leave the country immediately," a friend advised.

"Leave the country? Never! I am not a coward!"

"This government cannot continue like this. If I was you, I would leave. Better be a coward and alive than brave and dead…"

The last sentence shook him. 'Dead' while planning a life with Naomie?

Without much thought, Palomino made the decision to leave.

Naomie wanted to stay with him until the end. Despite the admonitions of her family, she was willing to take the risk.

Thus, on a summer night of August 1984, Palomino embarked on a flimsy sailboat called *Kanntèr* destined for Miami. Tears in their eyes, Naomie and Palomino could not let go of each other. On that frail boat one hundred and sixty impatient passengers were silent - no one dared to say a word, too afraid to break this sadly passionate embrace.

"Please! Let's go! The time is now!" cried out finally the "Captain".

Leaving each other's arms, inconsolable, Palomino mechanically slid into the boat. He had to live. He had to live for Naomie.

Naomie on the beach looked at the small sailboat, drifting away, and slowly disappearing in the darkness with half of herself on board. The refugees were now at God's mercy.

Palomino looked around. The need for survival had erased the social barriers. Intellectuals and ordinary people shared the same fate on this sailboat. The boat was poorly built and took on water several times. Palomino and a few other men used their bare hands to scoop water out. The winds had already tear the so-called sails. The boat was too small. People took turn to sit. Quickly, food and water became scarce. Only children had the priority. But, by an inexplicable miracle, no one lost their life.

After several days on the Windward Passage, a windy strait between Haiti and Cuba, and Chance as their only compass, the sailboat washed up on the coast of Miami. Palomino and the 160 others felt finally safe. The sky seemed bluer, the air fresher, and the sand softer than Haiti's.

Dirty and tired, Palomino got out of the boat and helped a few women to do the same. He took a few steps on the beach with the strength he had left, fell on his knees, and poured out his soul in tears. His life flashed before his eyes. His heart was missing the love he left behind.

But he must live, live for Naomie. Palomino dried his tears. Naomie's face gave him courage. He will work hard for her. He will work for the family they will have. No more fears. Their love will blossom like the Garden of Lovers they planted together…

CHAPTER 4

Voices frantically shouting brought Palomino back to reality. The American Coast Guards found the illegal migrants. The helicopter's loud noise above replaced hope with fear. They were all arrested, imprisoned, and cautioned to be repatriated.

Palomino did not understand what was happening. He never thought he could be sent back. In his mind, the United States was the country where he would solutioned all his problems. In his plans, he would legalize his situation, continue his work, make a lot of money, and bring to him the woman of his life…

The coast guards distributed food and provided medical care to whomever needed it. Palomino's arms and face were burnt by the sun and dried by the wind. The unlucky 160 were brought to a refugee camp already filled with other 'boat-people'. With interpreters at-hand, the custom agents conducted the usual interviews. A lot of those caught were denied legal residency. Desperate tears were heard everywhere.

Palomino's confusion heightened. A feeling of lost and abandonment invaded him while he waited. No interpreter could translate what he was feeling. Dried lips, haggard eyes reflected Palomino's acute pain. In forcing him to leave, the henchmen of the regime took everything away from him: love, sun, and country. What else could this wicked world offer him if not pain and desperation…

One day, Tamara, a young Haitian-American woman visited the camp. She worked for a religious institution that provided help to refugees. She has been living in Miami for 25 years.

Palomino's disheartened face attracted her attention.

"Young man, why are you crying like this?" she asked him. "Don't be bashful. Tell me your story. Maybe, I can help your case. You never know."

Tamara soft tone and her frank words comforted Palomino. The young man recounted his story from beginning to his present situation.

"Oh! My God! This is a difficult case. Do you have any relatives in Miami I can call?"

"No, I don't have any. I had a friend's number but I think I lost it at sea."

"I understand…Listen, I'm going to see what I can do. Meanwhile keep praying maybe you'll be heard."

From a plastic bag Palomino took out a copy of the New Testament.

"That's the only thing helping me right now", he said with conviction.

"That's good. Hope in the Lord. He will help you. On my side, I'll do everything I can to pull you out from the jaws of the lion. Don't be afraid. Be patient. I'll come back."

The young woman was decided. She will find an immigration attorney. Quickly, she understood that without some sort of papers nothing will happen for Palomino. Nonetheless, his case revigorated her. His dire situation made an impression on her and touched her sense of justice.

Tamara was acquainted with Attorney Brown. With the number of successful cases, he argued during the years, Attorney Brown and Tamara became good friends.

"Has he filled out the asylum request?"

"Yes. I helped him with it. He doesn't understand much English and the legal language of these papers is complicated."

Brown looked at Tamara directly in the eyes and said:

"I admire your tenacity young lady… But, you know, if you really want to save him there's only one alternative."

"Which is?"

"Marry him to stop the deportation."

"Marry a stranger!" Tamara cried out.

"You know how fast these cases are expedited. He doesn't have a lot of time. If the Immigration Services accept his story, it will take him years before he becomes legal. You must marry him immediately. That will stop the deportation. They will leave him alone. That's the only solution. There's no other."

"That's not reasonable."

"Listen," said Brown. "That's a role you'll have to play to stop the deportation.

You see...that's the only solution. Later, you could divorce him. It's that simple."

Tamara married Palomino. Tamara continued living with her parents and Palomino find refuge at one of her friends' house located in the area of Little Haiti.

Palomino could not stop thinking of Naomie. To relieve the stress, he wrote her letters explaining his situation. The many letters received no response. Palomino did not know what to think: was the pressure to much for Naomie? Has she forgotten him? With her talent and beauty, could have she found another suiter?

Unfortunately, the letters never reached Naomie in Haiti. Days after Palomino's departure, the Bourjoly family moved to escape possible persecutions. John, a young man living in the neighborhood, promised to take care of the house. He has been secretly in love with Naomie for a long time. In Palomino's absence, he used different ruses to win her over.

Receiving the mail, John made the separations. After reading Palomino's letters, he hid them. Each time, he assured the family that Palomino has not written. Naomie was despondent. How can their love have ended in such a way? Has he perished on the high seas? Has he found an American woman?

Denied longing convinced Naomie that Palomino forgot her. John was always there to hear her anxious thoughts. Sadness changed into irritation, incomprehension, and discouragement. John was always there with comforting words. Little by little, he became the consoler and confident. His wide shoulders were always ready to welcome her. John was emboldened so much by his new role that one day he asked her hand in marriage. Naomie was surprised by the request. Not one moment had she thought John had such feeling toward her. But Naomie loved Palomino. Her heart was beating only for him…

Little Haiti was a very animated place. The music, the food, the camaraderie, that Haitian library they just opened where he could discuss literature… everything in that suburb helped Palomino regain life.

Tamara was watching the evolution of Palomino. Attracted toward each other's personality, a beautiful friendship started to developed between them.

Palomino became a dishwasher in a restaurant in Miami. Every day he went to work with his head full of hope, not looking at his hands becoming callous, nor the little salary he was earning. Evenings, though tired, and after listening to the news of the country and the local Haitian community, Palomino was learning English from a book Tamara gave him. He aimed at studying and resuming his career of a journalist. Not one day, he did not write to Naomie long love letters about his present life and future dreams before going to bed…

Later, words of the dictator leaving power were announced. Palomino joined the crowds rejoicing in the streets of Little Haiti. He was no longer afraid. He could see the light at the end of the tunnel. As soon as he would receive residency, he would return to his country. Yes, he must return. All those letters without a single response… Something must have happened. He wanted to find out himself.

CHAPTER 5

The returning day finally arrived. Palomino was at the terminal hours before departure. It was only three years since he left.

"Don't worry," said Palomino to Tamara. "I'll pass on the message for you as soon as I arrive."

"Thank you. I'll let my aunt know…"

Palomino frowned while looking at Tamara.

"How can I thank you? I would have never been able to do any of this without you?"

"You were worth all the help you got," answered Tamara with tenderness.

"I will be forever grateful. I will never forget you."

Tamara stood on the tip of her toes and give him a tender kiss on his cheeks. The young woman could not resist the intellectual and physical charms of Palomino. Despite of herself, romantic feelings for him grew inside of her. Several times, she held back the desire to tell him because she knew his heart was elsewhere. When only Palomino decided to return, she mustered her courage and declared her deep love for him…

When the plane touched the Haitian soil, Palomino was first to unbuckle himself. The soothing Caribbean heat hit his face. He stopped for a moment at the landing gate feeling the sun and listening to the troubadour music welcoming the passengers. Once the immigration checkpoint formalities resumed, Palomino took a "Chaffeur-Guide" (a tourist taxi) and went straight to Naomie's former address.

The house looked different, abandoned. The garden had only dead flowers.

"Who are you looking for Sir?" asked the directly facing neighbor.

Palomino did not know her. He introduced himself and asked about Naomie's whereabouts.

"Naomie?" the lady replied. "You have the wrong address Sir. There's no Naomie here. The house has been abandoned for some time now. The people moved."

"Do you know where they live now?" Palomino asked.

"From what I heard they're living somewhere in Delmas but I don't know where exactly…There's only one young man that could have helped you. He was living next door. But it's been a few months since he got married and moved away also… Sorry…"

Naomie moved. That is why she has not been able to respond to the letters.

Palomino thanked the lady and got back in the taxi. The taxi dropped him off at a little hotel on the Delmas Boulevard. He did not want to visit his family yet. We wanted to stay incognito a few days to continue his search.

The country has changed. Presidential election was to be held soon. But growing insecurity made things worst. Palomino had no desire to be involved in politics right away. All he wanted was finding the woman of his life.

Palomino took the simplest room. Exhausted, he quickly fell asleep. At dawn the next day, he got up and put in a bag the item that Tamara gave him for her aunt. The aunt lived somewhere off the Delmas boulevard, Delmas 19. Palomino intended

50

to delay this errand as long as possible. His priority was finding Naomie. But how, without a fixed address?

The houses were succeeding after each other on the boulevard. They all looked the same. Palomino didn't know where to stop. Each time he would ask someone for information regarding the Bourjolys, no one knew them.

It was getting late. He had to deliver the item. When he entered Delams 19, he stopped for a few seconds in front of the Ciné Impérial, a movie theatre, where he and Naomie would often go back in the days to watch romantic movies that made Naomie cry…

After the errand, Palomino was returning to his hotel when the voice of a woman on a green painted balcony attracted his attention. The woman shouted some orders to someone below and disappeared.

The familiarity of that voice made Palomino's heart jump.

"Naomie!" he shouted.

Palomino crossed the street and knocked on the gate.

John was perplexed to see the knocking person was Palomino. Though, he took on a few pounds, was slightly gray on the temples, had a little mustache, he would still remember Palomino decades later.

Palomino greeted John and asked for Naomi.

John's demeanor changed. He became aggressive.

"What do you want exactly?" he asked defensively.

"She doesn't live here?" Palomino replied.

"She does. But what do you want?"

Palomino was surprised to see John and did not understand what he was doing at the Bourjolys.

"I need to speak with Naomie. Naomie Bourjoly," replied Palomino impatiently. "She lives here, right?"

John frowned, gave Palomino a dirty look, and went inside the house looking for his wife.

Naomie was shocked and trembling when she saw Palomino. Without a smile, she shouted:

"You? What brought you here? I'm dreaming! You go to Miami or New York, whatever! Not a letter to say 'I'm alive' or ask 'how I was doing'. Three years. THREE YEARS! You left me with all kinds of suffering. I hoped you would write me! But never! ..."

Palomino was quiet but shocked at Naomie's words. He left a slim, calm, and tender young lady. But now he was facing a rounder aggressive woman. Palomino just wanted to talk to Naomie. He wanted a chance to clear the air. He wanted a response to the passionate letters he sent. But Naomie did not want to hear anything. She was ferociously mad.

"What kind of man are you? A man with a heart of stone? What do you want? They even told me you were married. What are you doing in my house, Sir?"

Naomie's angry words became tearful. She turned around suddenly and rushed inside the house.

"I don't see the reason for all this noise in front of my house," intervened John gravely. "You're disturbing the woman! She's married!... So, Sir your presence is not welcomed! I urge you to leave. She doesn't want to talk to you. Leave!"

My house? Married? To whom? And how? These words resounded in Palomino's head. He suddenly remembered seeing a few times this John at Naomie's house and the way he looked at her bothered him more than once.

Palomino felt a rage slowly rising inside of him. How in such a little time Naomie forgot him in the arms of another? So, not only this man was waiting to take his place but also the hands of the woman he loves. And now without any hindrance, he was shooing him like a dog! Palomino was seeing red! From a few people, now the entire neighborhood was witnessing this domestic scene.

John called the police. They came quickly. They tried to reason with Palomino and finally forced him to leave.

With eyes full of sadness and indignation, Palomino took the direction of the hotel. He, whose heart full of happiness and lightness, was certain that day he would celebrate his love with his fiancée... And now, he just suffered the worst disappointment: rejection from the only one he loves. Who would imagine such a thing?

The tears streamed down his face. He walked, he walked until he lost his breath. At one point, he sat on the sidewalk… He could not understand what had just happened, what happened to Naomie, and how she treated him. Ah! If only he had a chance to explain!

After the incident build-up frustrations, indignations, and disillusions weighed heavily on Naomie's heart. She ran into the house because she could not process his presence in front of her.

Days later, images of the exchanges were still haunting her. The Police chasing Palomino gave her such a pain. This was not her dream. This was not what she had hoped for herself. More than once, she regretted not giving Palomino a chance to talk. She was still in love with him. But, when she heard the news of his marriage from a friend of Gertrude living in Miami, she lost all hope. She even became sick because of the pain she felt in her heart, in her soul.

Naomie was not in love with John. Yes, he was protective and attentive but he was not in her heart. Naomie's parents opposed the marriage because they knew that. But because of a frustrating wait, bad news, and her honor, she felt compelled to accept. She wanted to start anew and erase her pain…

When someone would pass Naomie on the streets, she would put up a smile on her face to hide the true despair she was feeling inside. But now she was pregnant with John's child. One must accept life as it comes. She had no choice. Like a French song says:

You take the train when the boat leaves
So that you are not alone on the bay
It's much better that way…

Gertrude's friend did not tell Naomie the whole story. The details of the marriage, of deportation threat, Naomie was told any of it. If only she received the letters and read them. John used all kinds of tricks to erase Palomino in her life. He encouraged Naomie to imagine the worse of Palomino. He forced her to entertain the idea that he forgot about her and that she is wasting her time waiting for him...

CHAPTER 6

Palomino decided to stay in Haiti. His family was surprised to see him three days after he had arrived. Explaining his reasons did not stop their criticisms: he stayed in hotel for three days. They would not accept that.

As time passed by, his family understood the incident between him and Naomie had a profound negative effect on him. Palomino was now suffering from depression and discouragement. He was lethargic. He did not sleep much, did not eat much, and often wrote love letters to his "fiancée".

He could not live without Naomie. Every day, he walked the streets like a crazed man. Despite medical treatment from the best specialists, his situation worsened. All Port-au-Prince was speaking of the downfall of the young man that came from a respected family, an educated man, the future of society…

Ah…miserable life!...

*

After Naomie's wedding, her parents left her the house on Delmas 19. They went to live with her older sister in a big house in Pétion-Ville. Gertrude's second pregnancy was difficult. Mrs. Bourjoly felt split between her two girls' pregnancies. She was relieved when Joséphine, who was studying nursing, offered her help.

On Naomie's last trimester, Joséphine came to live with her friend until the birth. Naomie recounted the latest events including Palomino's reappearance. Joséphine did her best not to talk again about that sad subject as it could affect Naomie's pregnancy.

The due date was fast approaching and Naomie needed still a few things. One day, after her husband left for work, Naomie took her car and drove to Pétion-Ville. Gertrude had just given birth to twins.

"My God!" Mrs. Bourjoly shouted seeing her daughter driving in her condition. "How can John let you drive like this?"

"Mom," said Naomie. "That's not a problem. Women nowadays are strong. We can't wait for our husbands to do everything for us."

"It's not about waiting. You could give birth while driving that car."

Mr. Bourjoly gave her daughter a kiss and a hug.

"Your mother is right Naomie. It's imprudent. Scott and Samuel could have come and pick you up."

Naomie dismissed her parents' admonitions. The twins were so beautiful. Despite Gertrude's difficult pregnancy, the actual birth was normal. She received a few advices for her sister. Time went by quickly. Naomie remembered suddenly that the store she wanted to go to will be closed soon. She quickly said goodbye.

Under a red light, on the other side of the streets, she saw a man, sitting on the sidewalk, talking to himself. He seemed lost in his own world unable to escape. This dirty man in rags looked strangely like Palomino.

Naomie trembled. She gave out a cry of horror. The lights changed. The traffic was dense and she could not turn around. People were honking. She had to go forward for a few kilometers before she could drive back to the intersection. When she finally did, the man was no longer there. Was he really Palomino in this unthinkable situation? She asked a man sitting on a wicker chair who the stranger might be.

"Palomino?" he repeated. "Ah! This crazy man! He just took a minibus."

So, it was him she saw earlier… This discovery affected the pregnant Naomie. She could no longer sleep. She could no longer eat. One day, taking advantage of the absence of Joséphine and her husband, she dressed herself up and filled two bags. One was full of food and the other of clothing. She threw one bag on her right shoulder and the other on the left. Her car being in disrepair at present would not stop her. Before leaving, she left instructions for Joséphine regarding the upcoming baby's shower.

Naomie was walking under the pressing sun though weighed down by three burden: a baby and two bags. She was determined to reach the place she saw Palomino earlier. She was unrelentless in her desire to find him, this man she so much loves.

"Palomino?" people repeated when she asked for information on the man. "Yes, we know him. You're family?"

"Yes," answered Naomie.

"He's always here normally. But not today...Keep looking for him. He may not be far from here."

They explained how he lost his mind when he found out the girl he loved was married. He walks the streets uttering her name. Naomie thanked them for the information.

She rounded the neighborhood twice searching for him. Finally, losing hope, she shared the food with some vagabond children playing marbles on the porch of an abandoned house. She suddenly felt the need to see her own childhood home.

"Odain street please," she said to a taxi driver she just flagged.

Naomie needed to relive the souvenir of Palomino in the "Garden of Lovers". The garden was so beautiful then.

When Naomie pushed the little gate, she sighed ghastly. Left without care, the house lost its luster. The paint was flaking and parts of the balustrade succumbed to the previous year's hurricane. She entered the courtyard and stood in the middle of the garden. Dead flowers and plants surrounded her. Even the bench, a witness to their amorous exchanges, was in state of dilapidation. The home that provided so much happiness, so many beautiful years, was in ruins…

Chapter 7

A week later, after lunch, in the dining room, Naomie was drinking a reinvigorating cup of coffee and listening to music on the radio. Joséphine entered and looked at her sadly.

"Naomie," she started slowly, "I must talk to you. But you must stay calm or I will not say anything."

"If you have something to say," replied Naomie, "say it."

"Ok…You remember when I had to clean the house for the party? Well, I went deep. I went all over. Carefully tucked in the closet of the baby's room was a small bag.

In the bag, I found a few letters that Palomino wrote to you while he was in Miami…"

Naomie's eyes widened.

"Go get these letters!" Naomie yelled with a dry throat.

She ripped open the letters. The more she read, the more lost she felt.

"My God, my God, my God!" she shouted. "Look what John did to me! He always assured me Palomino never wrote. He was lying!"

"Naomie!… Forget all of this!"

"Look at all these letters! Look! Look my God! I trusted him! He assassinated me! He assassinated Palomino! He pitted us against each other! John is a wicked man, a criminal! I will make him pay!"

Joséphine tried to calm Naomie down.

"Think of your coming baby! Calm down!"

"Calm down? Don't you see John's crime? I trusted him so much!"

While Naomie was wrestling with those thoughts, the midday headline news came on the radio.

'A man was critically injured when, under the influence of alcohol, he fell off a cliff on hilly Nazon road. The Police and the Red Cross are on the scene. He is in an uncertain state. It is reported that he is constantly uttering the name: Naomie, Naomie, Naomie.'

The letters slid off Naomie's hands and spread on the floor. Barefoot, in bedroom clothes, hair undone, Naomie grabbed on the table her car keys.

"Naomie! No!" said firmly Joséphine while blocking her way.

"Leave me alone! Let me go!"

Strengthened by love, she pushed Joséphine on the side and her friend fell on the ground. She rushed to the car. She took the direction of the General Hospital.

She sped up under the yellow lights, raced by cars and people on Lalue Street. Stunned walkers were running for fear of a mad woman. She stopped at no intersections. Tears were blurring her vision and tightening her throat. The more she sped, the more the road seemed long. Naomie had a premonition something bad was going to happen. She wanted to arrive to the hospital before it was too late.

Not far from the hospital, between the streets of Saint-Honoré and Oswald Durand, she lost control of the car and hit a pole. People hurried to help the woman driver. But not realizing the situation and blinded by one thought, one thought alone, she swung open the car door, and ran toward the hospital. She ran frenzied! She ran desperately! She ran with a hand on her heart!

Out of breath, she was inside the hospital finally.

"Palomino!" she said franticly.

"Palomino…" repeated the receptionist.

"The man in the Nazon accident!" she emphasized.

The receptionist felt a certain compassion looking at the pregnant woman.

"This way Ma'am," the receptionist said while holding her by the arm.

Palomino was stretched on the hospital bed all bloodied. His head, his face, his arms, his legs, his torso were all bandaged. Naomie uttered a horrifying cry.

"Palomino, Palomino don't die! It's Naomie! Open your eyes, open your eyes! You cannot die like this, Palomino! Talk to me, Palomino! You cannot die like this!"

Patients and patients' families turned to look at that pregnant woman pleading desperately to an agonizing man not to die.

"It's Naomie! The woman you loved so much! It's me! Open your eyes! Please, make an effort! I know everything now! I know what happened! It's not your fault! It's not my fault! Let's forget, Palomino! Let's forget! Talk to me! Talk to me! Open your eyes!"

Palomino opened his eyes slightly with a light smile on his lips.

"I Love You Naomie…"

These were his last words. He was gone. Naomie hugged him. Tears bursting, she was uncontrollable. The sound of a deep pain came from her entire body. She cried to total exhaustion.

A deafening silence fell on the room. The attending nurses realized that Naomie was not moving, was no longer crying. They hastened to her side.

She too was gone.

She too closed her eyes.

The doctors on duty realized she was pregnant and wanted to save the baby. The baby's heart was still beating strongly. Naomie was dashed to the operating room.

It was a girl. Natacha...

CHAPTER 8

Not being able to stop Naomie, Joséphine called the entire family. John, Mr. Bourjoly, Samuel, Scott, and herself arrived at the hospital almost at the same time.

John collapsed with the news of his wife's death. Only a few days ago, they celebrated the expected arrival of Natacha. Naomie was so beautiful, so happy, so vivacious then…

Mr. Bourjoly was holding his head between his hands. How is he going to tell his wife the passing of their daughter, their dearest Naomie?

Scott, normally an arrogant teenager of 17, was crying like a child on the shoulders of Samuel. Joséphine was the only stoic one.

A nurse took Josephine to the nursery. Natacha weighed 6½ pounds and seemed ready for life. Josephine took the baby in her arms and whispered into her hears:

"I will take care of you…"

The lovers were cemented in life and death. They were buried on the same day, side by side in a cemetery not far from the Bourjoly's old house.

And that's how their story ended…

*

It was unheard of - two young people died because they loved too much. All their dear ones, their families including children and adults, everyone were lamenting their departure…

Ah friends, courage! Maybe, that is the way it was meant to end.

God will have the last word because Palomino and Naomie did nothing wrong. They were spreading nothing but love…

One day we will take the same road. Yesterday was their time, tomorrow will be ours.

Ah, courage! Maybe, that is the way it was meant to end…

CHAPTER 9

But, wait! This may not be the end of the story.

And how, you may be asking?

God did not play his last note in this symphony.

This young man and that young woman did nothing wrong. They were spreading nothing but love…

Well, you remember Tamara, right? Remember before Palomino went back to Haiti, Tamara finally avowed her love to him. Well, well, well! A few weeks after his departure, Tamara found out she was pregnant. Palomino knew nothing of it. She had a boy whom she named after the father: Palomino Junior.

Though the tragedy of Palomino and Naomie spread all around Port-au-Prince, Tamara's aunt never heard of it.

Years later, Tamara learned of what happened. It was painful for her. She did not have even a picture of Palomino. Beside the memories, she had nothing to show her son. She decided to travel to Haiti to present him to her own family and that of Palomino's.

Tamara was happy to rediscover the country she left a long time ago when she was just a youngster. Her parents and Palomino had often talked about Haiti's simple life.

Tamara and her son were warmly accepted. Every day family members would come to see the child that looked so much like his father.

Tamara's two weeks' vacation were coming to an end. But she wanted to see where Palomino was buried. On the eve of her departure, she went with her son onto his tomb's sight. On that day, John also brought his daughter to her mother's tomb sight. Joséphine came along.

Tamara saw them. She greeted them silently. She put down a bouquet of flowers on Palomino's tomb and turned to leave. But the children would not let them. It has been a while since they became instant friends.

They came in the world the same day, the same year, almost at the same hour. They both were two years old.

They forced the parents to talk to each other.

"This is Natacha. Naomie's daughter," said John.

"Ah. She's beautiful," answered Tamara. "This is Palomino Junior, the son of Palomino."

John was surprised. He did not know that Palomino had a child. He examined the boy and agreed he looked just him, Palomino, the man he destroyed the life of and consequently that of his wife.

The children did not want to leave each other. Countering the insistences of their parents, they started to cry.

"Well," John said. "I must invite you for coffee."

The children had other ideas. Joséphine proposed to see what they had in mind and to follow them.

They took the road to the Bourjoly's old house. They were walking happily. The adults were following. They walked directly where Palomino and Naomie met - there among the flowers where they exchanged words in the Garden of Lovers.

Remember the dead flowers that welcomed Naomie the last time she was looking for Palomino. When the children crossed the gate, a few flowers were blossoming again. They were so beautiful!

Wherever Naomie and Palomino walked, talked, sat, and lived their love, the children played there.

The next day, Tamara returned to Miami with Palomino Junior. Their children demanded that they keep in touch. The distance between them did not exist. Palomino Junior was sad that he could not see Natacha. The passing months did not erase her in his mind.

Tamara's parents desired for a long time to retire in their country of origin. The little house they were building in Haiti was nearing completion. Seeing the sadness of their only grandson, they asked Tamara to come with them and stay. She accepted.

Palomino Junior and Natacha were meeting once again.

They went to the same school, same university, and grew up together. As expected, they fell in love with each other and married where their parents met for the first time.

What wedding ceremony!

What wonderful party!

People danced, ate, and celebrated!

A memorable wedding!

Well, it is in this way God continued the idyllic relation of Palomino and Naomie.

And this time, it was for real.

About the Author

Born in Haiti, Paul M. Polynice has been living in the United-States for a number of years.

The Story of Us (*Histoire de Nous*) is his first published novel.

www.ingramcontent.com/pod-product-compliance
Lightning Source LLC
Chambersburg PA
CBHW072358190626
46811CB00019B/1393